The Broken Lighthouse

by James Messina

Marker Kid Children's Books
markerkid.com

First Edition: May 2014
Printed in the United States of America
ISBN: 9780692212035

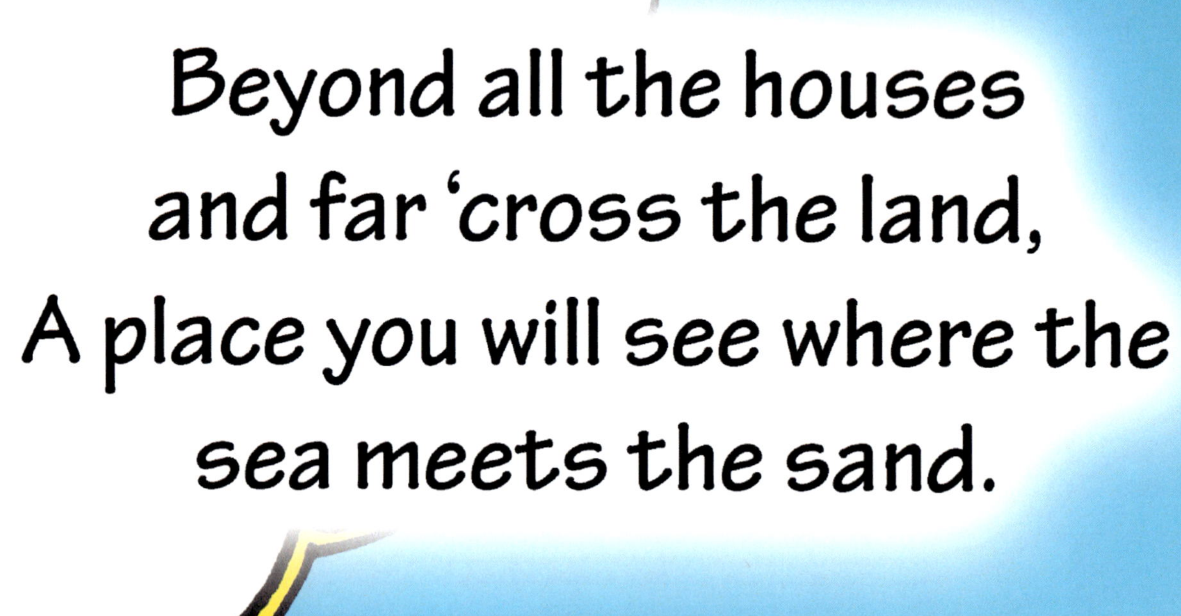

Beyond all the houses
and far ‘cross the land,
A place you will see where the
sea meets the sand.

And there, on the shore,
looking down on the view,
Is a beautiful lighthouse -
that lighthouse is YOU!

Each morning you wake to
the soft ocean breeze,
The sound of the waves and
the smell of the seas.

The clouds float their paths
and the birds sing their song,
And you feel as though nothing
could ever go wrong.

But one day you might
feel a change in the wind-
-The air somewhat colder, the
light somewhat dimmed.

And then you might see
a new cloud 'cross the bay,
A storm is approaching and
dark'ning the day.

But you are a lighthouse
and that's what you do:
Light up the world
till the darkness is through.

But this time you find
something terribly wrong,
You try and you try
but your light won't go on!

Then darkness will gather
to block out the sun.
The darkness is thick
and it sure isn't fun.
And try as you will with your
strength and your size,
You'll learn that sometimes
you can't stop stormy skies.

A gust of wind, howling,
will come passing by,
Raging and spooky
and close it will fly.

Oh how you'll wish
from your toes to your top,
That the wind
blowing fiercely and fast
would just stop.

Then waves will appear
in the midst of the storm,
So giant and tow'ring
in strength and in form,

Rising up quickly
and crashing back down.
You'll probably fear,
and you'll probably frown.

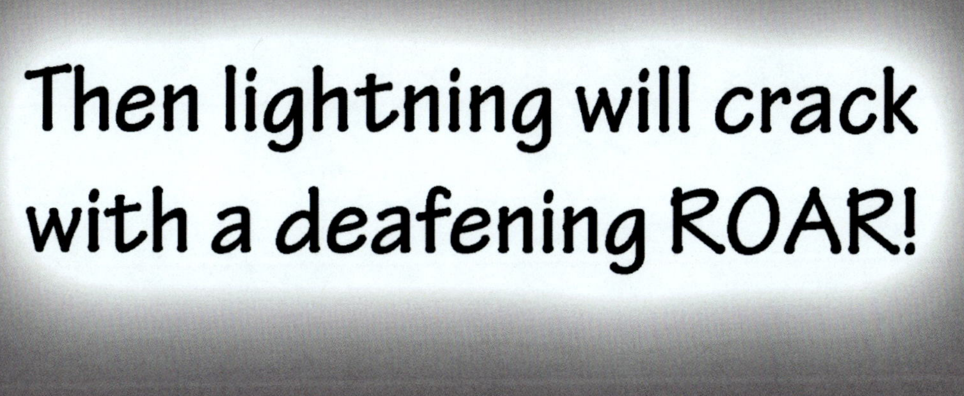

Then lightning will crack
with a deafening ROAR!

And right at that moment
the rain starts to POUR!
You'll feel all alone
in that miserable place,
With lightning and darkness,
and rain on your face.

But just when it
seems that there's
no hope in sight,
You see a small
man coming near,
through the night.

He walks up to you
and you then hear him say,
“Don’t worry lighthouse,
it’ll all be okay.”

He climbs up halfway
but he doesn't stop there,
He climbs and he climbs
to the top of the stair.
He takes out a toolbox
and to your delight,
He twists and he turns
till he fixes the light!

The light will then make you
so happy indeed.
From darkness so endless
and cruel you'll be freed.

Chasing the storm
and the darkness away-
Replaced with the shine
of a bright golden spray.

Then on the horizon
you'll see a faint glow.
The sun is returning
and shining below.

The dark clouds will scatter
and get on their way,
And make space for light
again - beautiful day!

And soon all the darkness
will give way to dawn,
And in the warm sun
you will feel you belong.

Glad you will be that you
patiently waited.
Then shedding a tear
you will shout,
"I have made it!"

THE END

38989896R00019

Made in the USA
Lexington, KY
14 May 2019